HOCKEY SUPERSTARS

TOP Rookies

NHL®

BY

James Duplacey

Kids Can Press

TORONTO

Kids Can Press Ltd. acknowledges with appreciation the assistance of the
Canada Council and the Ontario Arts Council in the production of this book.

Canadian Cataloguing in Publication Data

Duplacey, James
Top rookies

Includes index.
ISBN 1-55074-252-3

1. National Hockey League — Biography — Juvenile literature.
2. Hockey players — Biography — Juvenile literature. I. Title. II. Series.

GV848.5.A1D8 1995 j796.962'092'2 C95-930785-0

Kids Can Press Ltd.
29 Birch Avenue
Toronto, Ontario, Canada
M4V 1E2

Edited by Elizabeth MacLeod
Book design and electronic page layout by First Image
Printed and bound in Hong Kong

95 0 9 8 7 6 5 4 3 2 1

Photo credits
Bruce Bennett Studios: cover (left, second from left, second from right, right, centre front), 3 (left, second from right, right), 4 (top left, bottom left), 5 (all), 6 (both), 7 (both), 8 (both), 9 (both), 11 (top left and centre), 12, 14 (both), 15 (all), 16 (both), 17 (both), 18, 20 (both), 21 (both), 22 (both), 24 (left), 25 (both), 27 (top left and right), 28 (both), 29 (top, bottom right), 30 (left), 31 (both), 32 (both), 33 (both), 34, 35 (both), 36, 40 (left, centre), back cover (left, right). **Tony Biegun/The Ice Age:** 19 (top left, bottom), 37 (top left). **Robert Binder Jr./Lovero Group:** 40 (right). **Hockey Hall of Fame:** 3 (second from left), 10 (left), 13 (right), 30 (right), 38. **Imperial Oil Turofsky Collection/Hockey Hall of Fame**: 23 (all), 39 (top and bottom left). **Doug MacLellan/Hockey Hall of Fame:** 4 (top right), 19 (top right), 24 (right), 26, 27 (bottom), 29 (bottom left), 37 (bottom left, right), back cover (centre). **Frank Prazak/ Hockey Hall of Fame:** cover (centre back), 4 (bottom right), 10 (right), 11 (top right, bottom), 13 (left), 39 (right).

CONTENTS

INTRODUCTION		4
COURAGE AND CHARACTER:	Jagr, Arnott	6
THE NEW WAVE:	Makarov, Yashin, Fedorov, Mogilny	8
ABOVE THE CROWD:	Orr	10
FRANCHISE PLAYERS:	Lemieux, Béliveau	12
THE RECORD BREAKERS:	Bossy, Nieuwendyk, Juneau	14
THE GREAT DEFENDERS:	Leetch, Murphy	16
THE FINNISH FLASH:	Selanne	18
HIGH-SCHOOL HEROES:	Carpenter, Lawton, Housley, Barrasso	20
COOL IN THE CREASE:	Brodeur, Sawchuk	22
MUSCLE AND MIGHT:	Clark, Chelios	24
THE RUSSIAN ROCKET:	Bure	26
STRENGTH AND STAMINA:	Potvin, Bourque	28
AGAINST THE ODDS:	Ridley, Voss, Dryden, Larmer	30
EUROPEAN INVASION:	Salming, Stastny	32
GOALTENDING GREATS:	Belfour, Esposito	34
THE COMPLETE PACKAGE:	Lindros	36
HALL OF FAME LEGENDS:	Apps, Geoffrion	38
FUTURE PHENOMS:	Friesen, Harvey, Kariya	40

Waiting ...

The rookie sits on the bench, nervously adjusting his gloves, his helmet, his skates. He could hardly sleep last night as he played this scene over and over again in his mind. His first National Hockey League game. Suddenly — finally — he feels a tap on his shoulder and sees the nodding glance of the coach. It's his turn. His time. He leaps over the boards. He feels as if every eye in the arena is on him as the linesman drops the puck and the game continues. For the rookie, work is just beginning. Getting to the NHL was one thing, now he has to prove that he belongs.

Every year, dozens of rookies have this chance. But only a handful go on to become stars. The hockey players in this book all experienced that fear of failure. But they quickly proved that they belonged in the NHL. They are all top rookies.

The NHL's rookie-of-the-year receives the Frank Calder Memorial Trophy. To qualify as a rookie, a player must be younger than 26 years of age. The player also must not have played more than 25 NHL games in any single preceding season or six or more games in any two preceding seasons. Teemu Selanne (above) won the award in 1993 and Bobby Orr (below) won it in 1967.

Phil Housley was a top rookie and is still a top-scoring defenceman.

Sergei Fedorov was only the seventh rookie in the history of the Detroit Red Wings to score 30 goals.

Since Mario Lemieux (above) won the Calder Trophy in 1985, an extra layer has been added to the trophy to hold all the winners' names. You can see it in the photo of Pavel Bure (below right), the 1992 Calder winner.

Ken Dryden won the Stanley Cup with Montreal before he won the Calder Trophy. How? He played less than 25 NHL games in his Cup-winning season — see the Calder Trophy rules on the facing page.

With each profile you'll see the player's rookie-season statistics. Here's how to read them:

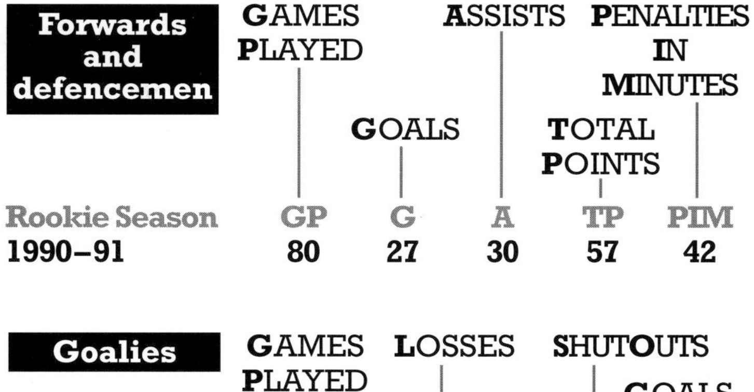

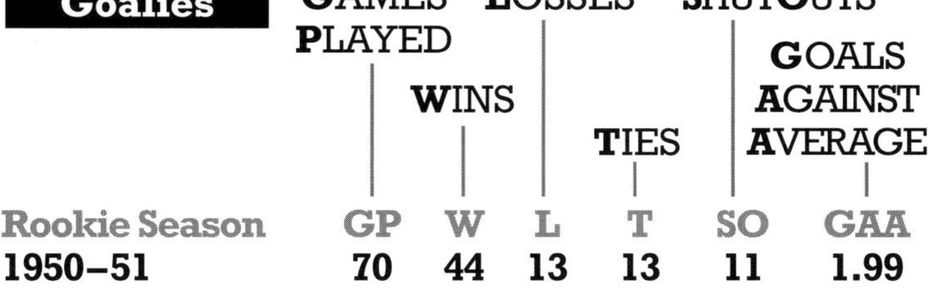

The teams listed in the stats are all the NHL teams the player has played on, not just his rookie-season teams.

Courage and Character

Jaromir Jagr

Right Wing — Pittsburgh

Rookie Season	GP	G	A	TP	PIM
1990–91	80	27	30	57	42

Jaromir Jagr was the first player from a Communist country to leave his homeland, Czechoslovakia, and attend the NHL Entry Draft. He was the fifth overall choice, and with his long, flowing hair and stylish skating, Jagr became an immediate fan favourite in Pittsburgh. His dazzling stickhandling and timely scoring helped the Penguins win their first Stanley Cup title in his rookie season.

In 1993–94, Jagr led the Penguins in scoring and has been chosen to represent the team in three consecutive All-Star games. But he doesn't forget his homeland. It was 1968 when soldiers marched into Czechoslovakia to enforce Communist rule, so Jagr wears number 68 on his sweater.

"Jaromir is an excellent skater who can kill penalties and forecheck well. He's a terrific competitor who comes up with a big game when needed."
NHL Central Scouting Bureau, 1990

Jagr became the youngest Penguin in team history to record a hat trick, scoring three goals in a 6–2 win over Boston on February 2, 1991, when he was just 18 years old.

Jason Arnott

Centre — Edmonton

Rookie Season	GP	G	A	TP	PIM
1993–94	78	33	35	68	104

It is very rare for a player in his first NHL season to become a team leader. But Jason Arnott is not your average rookie. He proved early in the 1993–94 season that he was a "character" player. That means he can motivate his teammates in the dressing room and lead by example on the ice. After only three months with the Oilers, Arnott was appointed the team's alternate captain.

Arnott impressed fans with his willingness to battle for the puck in the corners and take punishment in the slot. In his rookie year he was the team leader in shooting percentage and was second in power-play goals. Arnott's quick, accurate shot also helped him lead the club in goals and he won a spot on the NHL's All-Rookie Team.

"In mini-camp, he was head and shoulders above everybody else. Best of all, he's got mental toughness, and that's what will make him great."

TED GREEN, 1993
Edmonton Oilers coach

Arnott is one of only three Edmonton Oilers to be selected to the NHL's All-Rookie Team.

THE NEW WAVE

Sergei Makarov

Right Wing — Calgary, San Jose

Rookie Season	GP	G	A	TP	PIM
1989–90	80	24	62	86	55

The Russian new wave began with Sergei Makarov. A member of the Moscow Red Army's famed K-L-M line with Vladimir Krutov and Igor Larionov, Makarov was named the Soviet Player of the Year three times. He was the first Russian-born player to make an impact in the NHL, and he became the first to win an NHL award when he captured the Calder Trophy as top rookie.

"He's got great ability to go to the net. And he's very effective in the corners. The thing about him is that he always finds a way to improvise."
Dave King, 1987
Canadian National Team coach

Alexei Yashin

Centre — Ottawa

Rookie Season	GP	G	A	TP	PIM
1993–94	83	30	49	79	22

Alexei Yashin is part of the NHL's new wave because he was ready to be an NHL star in his first season. While many young players need time in the minors, Yashin was already a proficient passer, swift skater and skilled shooter. In his rookie year he led Ottawa in six categories, including power-play goals, game-winning goals and short-handed goals. He also scored the game-winning goal in the 1994 All-Star Game.

"Alexei is a productive scorer with good, fast hands. He's clever, playing a smart finesse game with authority. He's powerful and never stops trying."
NHL Central Scouting Bureau, 1992

Sergei Fedorov

Centre — Detroit

Rookie Season	**GP**	**G**	**A**	**TP**	**PIM**
1990–91	**77**	**31**	**48**	**79**	**66**

Sergei Fedorov surprised many experts by adapting so easily to North American hockey. This Russian star's speed and finesse meshed perfectly with the Red Wings' aggressive offensive attack. In his first season Fedorov led all NHL rookies in scoring and he was named to the NHL/Upper Deck All-Rookie Team.

"Sergei was sensational as a rookie at the IIHF World Championships in 1989. He is the centre around whom the next Soviet super line will be built."

Goodwill Games Press Guide, 1990

Alexander Mogilny

Right Wing — Buffalo

Rookie Season	**GP**	**G**	**A**	**TP**	**PIM**
1989–90	**65**	**15**	**28**	**43**	**16**

When Alexander Mogilny joined the Sabres in 1989 he was just 20 years old and he was the youngest Russian-born player to skate in the NHL. In 1992–93 Mogilny scored 76 goals, the highest total ever for a Russian-born player in NHL history. Then in 1993–94 he became the first Russian player to serve as team captain, replacing Pat LaFontaine when he was injured.

"Alex is still learning what he can and can't do in this league. I've never played with anyone who can beat you in so many ways."

Pat LaFontaine, 1994
Teammate

Above the Crowd

Bobby Orr

Defence — Boston, Chicago

Rookie Season	GP	G	A	TP	PIM
1966–67	61	13	28	41	102

Even before Bobby Orr played his first game in the NHL, hockey fans predicted that he would one day lead the Boston Bruins to the Stanley Cup. For three years while Orr played junior hockey, the Bruins waited for the talented defenceman to join the team. When he finally did arrive in 1966, no one was disappointed. The 18-year-old from Parry Sound was clearly an athlete who was above the crowd.

Orr changed the way defencemen played the game. Before Orr, most defencemen stayed in their own end of the ice. Orr could lead the attack into the offensive zone and then speed back into position to stop the opposition. He had spectacular acceleration, a bullet shot, and the hockey intelligence to always be in the right spot at the right time.

In his first season, 1966–67, Orr won the Calder Trophy and was named a Second Team All-Star. His 41 points that season were second among NHL rearguards and his 13 goals led all defencemen. And he only got better! He won the Norris Memorial Trophy for being the NHL's best defenceman eight years in a row.

Orr went on to help the Bruins win two Stanley Cup titles. He also became the only defenceman to lead the NHL in scoring, a feat he accomplished twice. When he retired in 1979, he became one of only six players ever inducted into the Hockey Hall of Fame without having to serve the mandatory three-year waiting period.

Orr is one of only two defencemen in NHL history to be named MVP in the regular season three times.

"He has a God-given talent. In all the years I've been in hockey, I've never seen a prospect like Bobby Orr. He can do just about anything."
Hap Emms, 1966
Boston Bruins general manager

Orr was the first Boston Bruins defenceman to win the Calder Trophy.

Not only was Orr a leader on the power play but he was also a solid defender in his own zone.

Franchise Players

Mario Lemieux

Lemieux was only the third rookie in NHL history to score 100 points in his first season.

Centre — Pittsburgh

Rookie Season	GP	G	A	TP	PIM
1984–85	73	43	57	100	54

When the Pittsburgh Penguins selected Mario Lemieux first overall in the 1984 Entry Draft, they felt they had acquired the player who could make them winners. They were right. With big number 66 in the lineup, the Penguins have won two Stanley Cup titles.

Lemieux's greatest asset is his versatility. He has the size to knock a player off the puck, then whip home a wrist shot. He can outrace any defender, and he has the reach to calmly stretch around a goalie and slide the puck into the empty net. Lemieux scored his first NHL goal on his first NHL shift and he went on to score 100 points in his rookie season — and capture the Calder Trophy.

Lemieux is only the second player in NHL history to win the Conn Smythe Trophy for playoff MVP two years straight. Although injury and illness have momentarily stalled his career, he remains the heart of the Pittsburgh Penguins.

"He's going to be a great player in this league for a long, long time."

Ed Johnston, 1984
Pittsburgh Penguins general manager

Jean Béliveau

Centre — Montreal

Rookie Season	**GP**	**G**	**A**	**TP**	**PIM**
1953–54	**44**	**13**	**21**	**34**	**22**

Jean Béliveau was a hockey superstar even before he played in the NHL. As a rookie in the Quebec Senior Hockey League in 1952–53, he became the fifth player in pro hockey history to score 50 goals in a season. The contract Béliveau signed in 1953 was the richest ever offered to a first-year NHL player and he went on to finish among the top ten scorers in nine of the next 11 seasons.

The key to Béliveau's style was his graceful skating. He could accelerate quickly to outrace his checkers and turn on a dime to evade opposing defencemen. But there was something else that made Béliveau a "franchise" player. He treated his fans with respect and was always a gentleman, on and off the ice. He is still considered one of hockey's greatest goodwill ambassadors.

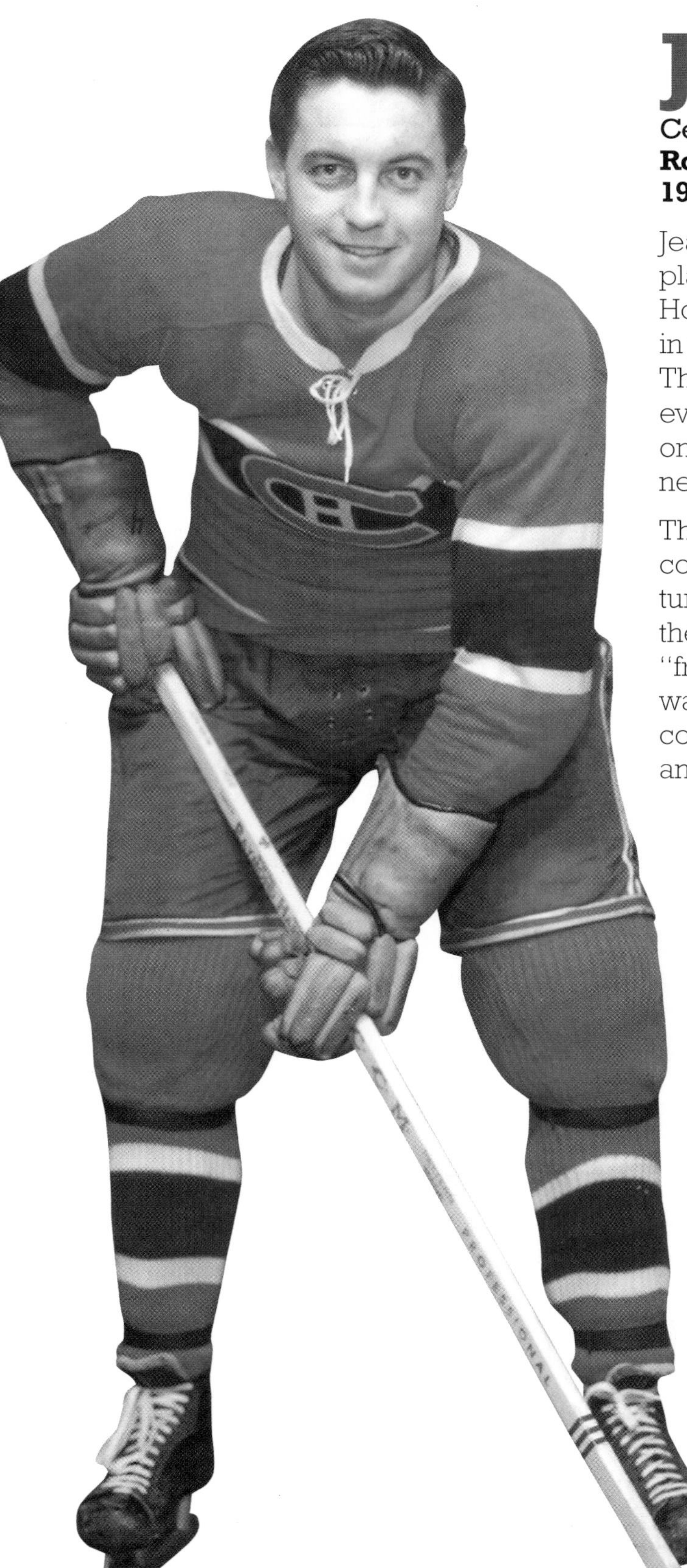

"He is a compelling figure on the ice, dwarfing the other players with his size, and dazzling them with his speed."
***LIFE* MAGAZINE, 1953**

Béliveau was captain of the Canadiens from 1961 to 1971 and played on ten Stanley Cup-winning teams.

The Record Breakers

Mike Bossy

Right Wing — NY Islanders

Rookie Season	GP	G	A	TP	PIM
1977–78	73	53	38	91	6

Many scouts overlooked Mike Bossy's talents. Fourteen other players were chosen before the Islanders drafted him in 1977. It was one of the wisest moves they ever made. With his deadly accurate wrist shot and lightning-quick release, Bossy set a rookie-season record of 53 goals and took the Calder. He went on to score at least 50 goals in nine straight seasons before retiring in 1987. Bossy was the first NHL player to score 50 goals while receiving less than ten minutes in penalties.

"He has tremendous puck sense. He always seems to know where the puck is coming from and where it's going."
***Newsweek* Magazine, 1978**

Joe Nieuwendyk

Centre — Calgary

Rookie Season	GP	G	A	TP	PIM
1987–88	75	51	41	92	23

Joe Nieuwendyk is only the second player in NHL history to score 50 goals in his rookie season. A crafty skater with quick hands, Nieuwendyk set four team rookie scoring records with Calgary and impressed everyone with his mature, intelligent play. He gives a full effort every time he's on the ice, and in 1991–92 he became the youngest captain in Calgary Flames history.

"He's big and tough and a good all-round player. He likes contact and that's important. He'll be a good solid player for the Flames."
Bob Johnson, 1987
Calgary Flames coach

Juneau set a Boston team record by scoring at least one point in his first 14 games of the 1992–93 season.

Joé Juneau

Centre/Left Wing — Boston, Washington

Rookie Season	GP	G	A	TP	PIM
1992–93	84	32	70	102	33

Only five players in NHL history have collected 100 points in their rookie season. Joé Juneau is one of them. Before joining the NHL, Juneau spent a season with the Canadian Olympic Team. That trained him to play under heavy pressure against top-level competition. Juneau brought that experience to the NHL, where he tied the NHL record for assists by a rookie. Juneau is a good passer, and while he may not look fast, he can really turn on the speed when he wants to.

"Joey's not a one-dimensional player. He plays a complete game at both ends of the rink."
Adam Oates, 1993
Teammate

The Great Defenders

Brian Leetch

Defence — NY Rangers

Rookie Season	GP	G	A	TP	PIM
1988–89	68	23	48	71	50

"I saw Bobby Orr at the same age, and I put Brian in the same breath as Orr. And I've never done that with anyone."
Phil Esposito, 1989
New York Rangers general manager

You might not expect a native of Texas to become one of the NHL's top defencemen, but Brian Leetch had an advantage over most boys. His father was a standout player at Boston College and he taught his son that in hockey mental preparation is as important as physical skill. Leetch learned his lessons well and has developed into one of the NHL's most gifted young players.

Leetch's puckhandling and defensive abilities have made him a three-time All-Star. In his rookie season, he led all rookies in points and assists and earned the Calder Trophy. Leetch won the Norris Trophy in 1992, and in 1994 he won the Conn Smythe Trophy and played on the Stanley-Cup winning New York Rangers. In 1993–94, Leetch helped guide the Rangers to the Stanley Cup title and became only the sixth defenceman to win the Conn Smythe Trophy.

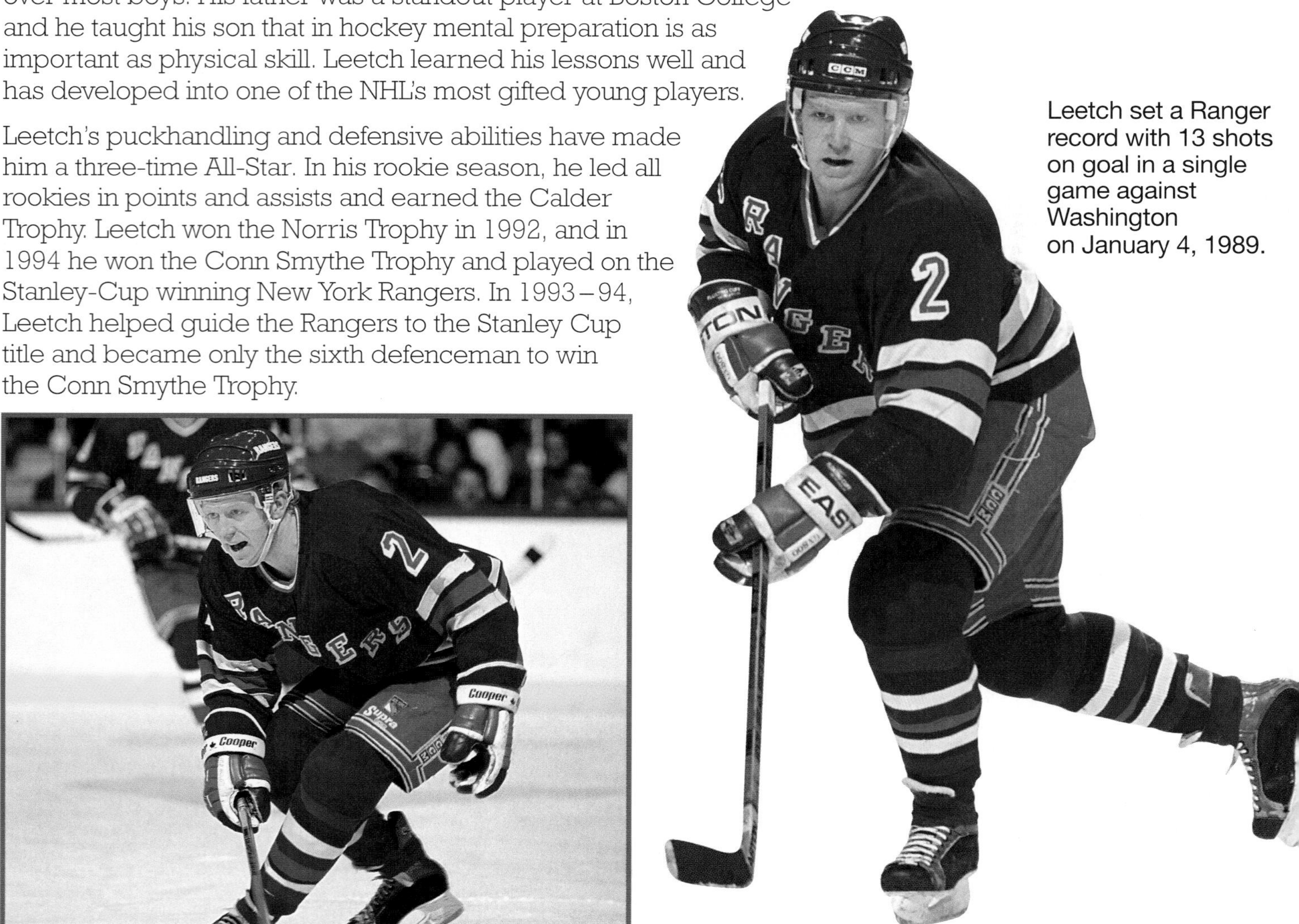

Leetch set a Ranger record with 13 shots on goal in a single game against Washington on January 4, 1989.

Larry Murphy

Defence — Los Angeles, Washington, Minnesota, Pittsburgh

Rookie Season	GP	G	A	TP	PIM
1980–81	80	16	60	76	79

Larry Murphy has quietly become one of the NHL's great defenders. He may not be as flashy as Brian Leetch or as well known as Ray Bourque, but "Murph" wears more Stanley Cup rings than either of them. Since his first year, when he set rookie records for assists (60) and points (76) by a defenceman, Murphy has been one of the NHL's steadiest performers.

Murphy's stylish skating and creative playmaking have won him a place on two All-Star teams in his 15-year career. This hard-working defenceman is also known for leading attacks and for his scoring ability on power plays. Murphy recorded a career-high 85 points in 1992–93 and is one of only six defencemen in NHL history to record 900 points.

Murphy won the Memorial Cup in 1979, the Stanley Cup in 1991 and 1992 and the Canada Cup in 1987 and 1991.

"He's a Stanley Cup defenceman. He not only has the body and the agility, he has the intelligence to direct a team on the ice. He's a winner who plays a very disciplined game."

Bob Berry, 1981
Los Angeles Kings coach

The Finnish Flash

Teemu Selanne

Right Wing — Winnipeg

Rookie Season	GP	G	A	TP	PIM
1992–93	**84**	**76**	**56**	**132**	**45**

A number of great hockey players from Finland have played in the NHL. However, none made the impact that Teemu Selanne did in his rookie season. Because of his quick hands and sensational hockey sense, he was called the Finnish Flash. And it didn't take long for Selanne to take the hockey world by storm. In 1992–93, he didn't just break the existing rookie records, he smashed them. In his first season in the NHL, Selanne scored 76 goals. Not only is that total the most ever by a rookie, it's the fifth highest in NHL history! He also set rookie records for points (132) and goals by a right-winger (76) and took rookie-of-the-year honours.

How could a rookie be so dominant? Selanne was very patient in preparing himself for his NHL career. Instead of coming to North America when he was drafted in 1988, he spent five more seasons playing in Finland. That extra time allowed him to mature both on and off the ice. When he finally did come to Winnipeg, he was ready to face the added pressure of playing in the NHL.

Selanne made the transition to the NHL style of play easily and he plays consistently strong hockey. Although he missed most of the 1993–94 season due to injuries, Selanne is still the player that makes the Jets fly.

As a rookie, Selanne established a Winnipeg team record by scoring at least one goal in nine straight game

NHL hockey is harder-hitting and is played on a smaller rink than the European hockey Selanne was used to playing.

> **"Teemu knows how to score big goals. He times his shots and passes very well and is adept at handling the puck with his skates."**
>
> **NHL CENTRAL SCOUTING BUREAU, 1988**

Selanne was a top rookie because he could be counted on to play well every night — most players take years to develop that consistency.

High-School Heroes

Bob Carpenter

Centre/Left Wing — Washington, NY Rangers, Los Angeles, Boston, New Jersey

Rookie Season	GP	G	A	TP	PIM
1981–82	80	32	35	67	69

Bob Carpenter is the first hockey player who had the talent and ability to go directly from playing high-school hockey to the NHL. His focus and concentration enabled him to play with the Washington Capitals as an 18-year-old in 1981–82. As a rookie, Carpenter finished fourth in team scoring with 32 goals and 35 assists. In 1984–85, he became the first American-born player to score 50 goals in a season.

"I saw Carpenter with forty of the best players in the United States, and he was the second youngest. He stood out like a neon light."

Steve Brklacich, 1981
St. Louis Blues director of player personnel

Brian Lawton

Left Wing — Minnesota, NY Rangers, Hartford, Quebec, Boston, San Jose

Rookie Season	GP	G	A	TP	PIM
1983–84	58	10	21	31	33

Brian Lawton caused headlines in 1983 when he became the first high-school player selected first overall in the NHL Entry Draft. He made the Minnesota roster because he had the ability to read the whole ice surface and react quickly. He also worked very hard on his special-team skills (power play and penalty killing). Lawton went on to become a premier defensive forward and played nine years in the NHL.

"Last year I was in high school, this year I'm playing against Gretzky, Doug Wilson and Denis Savard. I try to watch, learn and keep improving my quickness and endurance."

Brian Lawton, 1983

Phil Housley

Defence — Buffalo, Winnipeg, St. Louis, Calgary

Rookie Season	GP	G	A	TP	PIM
1982–83	77	19	47	66	39

It takes most defencemen years before they become regulars in the NHL. Not Phil Housley. He went straight from high school to the NHL. Although he is only 178 cm (5 feet 10 inches) tall, Housley's speed and his ability to learn quickly have helped him become an NHL star. He earned a berth on the NHL's All-Rookie Team, and went on to earn a place on the All-Star Team five times in a row.

Housley set a Buffalo rookie record with 47 assists in his first season.

Barrasso was the first American-born rookie to win the Calder Trophy since another goaltender, Frank Brimsek, won it in 1938–39.

Tom Barrasso

Goalie — Buffalo, Pittsburgh

Rookie Season	GP	W	L	T	SO	GAA
1983–84	42	26	12	3	2	2.84

A goaltender's most valuable quality is confidence. Tom Barrasso always knew he could play with the best. With his size, confidence and razor-sharp reflexes, Barrasso became the first goalie to jump directly from high school to the NHL. And he excelled. Barrasso was the first rookie since Tony Esposito to be a First Team All-Star and win both the Vezina Trophy and the Calder Trophy.

"He can rush the puck, he's an outstanding passer and he's creative. He has the knack for finding the open man, like an Orr or a Potvin, the great ones."

Scotty Bowman, 1982
Buffalo Sabres coach

"Tom was always very confident of his abilities. But let's face it, he wasn't proven wrong very often. We went 80-4-1 over the four years Tom played here."

Tom Fleming, 1983
High-school coach

Cool in the Crease

Martin Brodeur

Goalie — New Jersey

Rookie Season	GP	W	L	T	SO	GAA
1993–94	47	27	11	8	3	2.40

"Cool" is the best way to describe Martin Brodeur. Going into training camp in September 1993, he wasn't even expected to earn a job with the Devils, but he ended the season as the club's number-one goalie. Brodeur finished second in the NHL in the goals-against-average category and captured rookie-of-the-year honours.

However, it was in the pressure-packed playoffs that Brodeur really proved he was a future NHL star. This rookie led New Jersey to the Eastern Conference Finals before losing in double overtime to the eventual Stanley Cup winners, the Rangers. Brodeur is a stand-up goalie who is an expert at playing the angles and using his stick to intercept passes.

Brodeur established a New Jersey team record with a 1.95 goals-against average in the 1993–94 playoffs.

"The kid is solid, that's what I like from him. Even in the third period, with the other team all over us, he was right there. He's poised."

Jacques Lemaire, 1994
New Jersey Devils coach

Terry Sawchuk

Goalie — Detroit, Boston, Toronto, Los Angeles, NY Rangers

Rookie Season	GP	W	L	T	SO	GAA
1950–51	70	44	13	13	11	1.99

Terry Sawchuk had already won rookie-of-the-year awards in two minor leagues before making it to the NHL. But in the big league, he was even better. Thanks to his unique style of crouching down to see through the maze of sticks and skates in front of him, Sawchuk became the first goalie ever to win 40 games in one season — and that was in his rookie season! With his quick glove and fast feet, the rookie Sawchuk led the NHL in shutouts and earned the Calder Trophy.

Sawchuk was a man of endurance and courage. Despite hundreds of stitches and several serious injuries, he played for 21 years in the NHL. Sawchuk appeared in more games than any other goalie and set an all-time NHL record with 103 shutouts.

"He has big hands, fast reflexes, and an unorthodox gorilla-like crouch. And he may be the greatest hockey goalie ever."
LIFE MAGAZINE, 1952

Sawchuk won the Vezina Trophy four times in his career and won 435 games, an NHL record.

Muscle and Might

Wendel Clark

Left Wing — Toronto, Quebec

Rookie Season	GP	G	A	TP	PIM
1985–86	66	34	11	45	227

Even as a rookie, Wendel Clark was called a throwback to the early days of hockey. That's because he plays the game the way it used to be played: with muscle and might. Clark delivers blistering body-checks to any skater who comes near him and even old-timers say his wrist shot is one of the best they've ever seen.

Clark never wastes a shift. Every time he's on the ice, he's either crunching an opponent against the boards or racing full-out to reach a loose puck. In his first season, Clark scored 34 goals and was selected to the NHL's All-Rookie Team. As Toronto's captain he was one of the most popular players to ever wear a Maple Leafs uniform.

"He's a tough kid, an excellent hitter and an excellent skater. He's capable of taking the puck and going coast-to-coast any time he gets it."

Daryl Lubiniecki, 1985
Saskatoon Blades general manager

Clark's 34 goals as a rookie is a Maple Leaf record.

Chris Chelios

Defence — Montreal, Chicago

Rookie Season	GP	G	A	TP	PIM
1984–85	74	9	55	64	87

Chris Chelios is a gritty, in-your-face defenceman who uses all of his strength to win. Whether it's throwing his weight around or rushing the puck from end-to-end, Chelios gets results. He's one of the hardest-hitting defencemen in the NHL and he doesn't back down from anyone. Chelios is also known for his ability to clear the opposing team's forwards away from his team's goal. He also has a fierce pride in his team and his teammates.

In his rookie season, Chelios led all first-year defencemen in scoring and earned a spot on the NHL's All-Rookie Team. Since his debut in 1984, he has won the Norris Trophy twice and won the Stanley Cup with Montreal in 1986.

Chelios was the first Montreal Canadien defenceman to earn a berth on the League's All-Rookie Team.

"I just wanted to do well and break into the lineup. There's pressure everywhere, I guess, but I didn't feel there was any extra on me."

CHRIS CHELIOS, 1985

THE RUSSIAN ROCKET

Pavel Bure

Right Wing — Vancouver

Rookie Season	GP	G	A	TP	PIM
1991–92	**65**	**34**	**26**	**60**	**30**

Pavel Bure was one of the most dynamic rookies to ever play in the NHL when he joined the Vancouver Canucks in 1991–92. With his explosive speed and creative moves, he became an instant fan favourite. He quickly became known as the Russian Rocket because of his skating ability and his exciting end-to-end rushes.

In his rookie season, Bure played all three forward positions for the Canucks and showed he could be a leader both on and off the ice. He became the first Vancouver player to win a major NHL award, taking home the Calder Trophy as the NHL's top rookie. He led the Canucks with 34 goals, including six game-winners.

It's no surprise that Bure became a star athlete. His father was a champion swimmer who competed in three Olympics for the Soviet Union and he taught Pavel the importance of training and conditioning. The Russian Rocket followed his father's advice and became one of the NHL's superstars.

In 1993–94, Bure scored 60 times to become the first Russian-born player to lead the NHL in goals scored. He also helped lead Vancouver to the Stanley Cup finals. The best is definitely yet to come for the Russian Rocket.

In 1991–92, Bure led all rookie scorers with three short-handed goals and tied for the lead in the NHL with seven game-winning goals.

"I didn't make him run or lift weights for three hours a day, but I made sure he had focus. I told him that if you do something, do it to be the best."

Vladimir Bure, 1991
Father

Bure was so popular that even before he played in the NHL thousands of fans turned up to watch his first practice in Vancouver.

Strength and Stamina

Denis Potvin

Defence — NY Islanders

Rookie Season	GP	G	A	TP	PIM
1973–74	77	17	37	54	175

From a very early age, Denis Potvin was compared to Bobby Orr. Like Orr, he had the strength to play junior hockey against boys much older and bigger. And like Orr, he had the stamina to keep learning and improving. Potvin could rush the puck out of his own zone, slam on the brakes to sidestep an opponent and drive to the net to set up a scoring play. He joined the Islanders in 1973–74, and gave the team the dominant defenceman it needed to become one of the NHL's top clubs.

In his first season, Potvin finished fourth in scoring among all NHL defencemen and took rookie-of-the-year honours. Potvin went on to play top-level hockey for 15 years and he appeared in 1060 NHL games. He was the first defenceman to collect 1000 career points.

Potvin led the Islanders to four straight Stanley Cup titles in the 1980s.

"My personal goals are team goals. Respectability, winning, a positive attitude. I'll produce and I'll keep on learning."

Denis Potvin, 1973

Ray Bourque

Defence — Boston

Rookie Season	GP	G	A	TP	PIM
1979–80	80	17	48	65	73

From the moment he first stepped on the ice for the Boston Bruins in 1979–80, it was clear Ray Bourque would be a star. He combined good hockey sense with strong skating and a booming, accurate shot. In his first season he played all 80 games, won the Calder Trophy and became the first rookie rearguard in NHL history to be named a First Team All-Star.

As his career progressed, Bourque also proved he had the strength and stamina to play a long time in the NHL. Thanks to a strict off-ice training program, Bourque has been an All-Star in every one of his 15 NHL seasons and he holds the Bruins' record for games played by a defenceman. He's also one of the special group of NHLers who have scored over 1000 points.

"Ray is a magician. He can do tricks with the puck. He's learning all the time and he's getting better all the time. He'll be one of the dominant players in this league."

Brad Park, 1980
Seven-time NHL All-Star defenceman

Bourque is a five-time winner of the Norris Trophy as the NHL's top defenceman.

Against the Odds

Mike Ridley

Centre — NY Rangers, Washington, Toronto

Rookie Season	GP	G	A	TP	PIM
1985–86	80	22	43	65	69

While many Canadian hockey players go to colleges in the United States, Mike Ridley proved that athletes can continue their education in Canada and still become NHL stars. Ridley played for the University of Manitoba and collected 147 points in just 76 games. The Rangers signed him, and with his timely offence and steady defence Ridley went on to lead the team in scoring and earn a spot on the NHL's All-Rookie Team.

"Mike's made productive goal-scorers out of everyone he's played with. He has good passing skills, and, boy, is he durable. He comes out of every contact situation vertical."

Reg Higgs, 1985
New York Rangers assistant coach

Carl Voss

Centre — Toronto, Detroit, NY Rangers, Ottawa, St. Louis Eagles, NY Americans, Montreal Maroons, Chicago

Rookie Season	GP	G	A	TP	PIM
1932–33	48	8	15	23	10

Carl Voss was a perfect example of the saying, if at first you don't succeed, try, try, try again. He played his first NHL game in the 1926–27 season but spent the next seven years back in the minors before he earned a steady NHL job in 1932–33. Voss was named rookie-of-the-year the first year that honour was awarded and later became the NHL's first head referee. He was elected to the Hockey Hall of Fame in 1974.

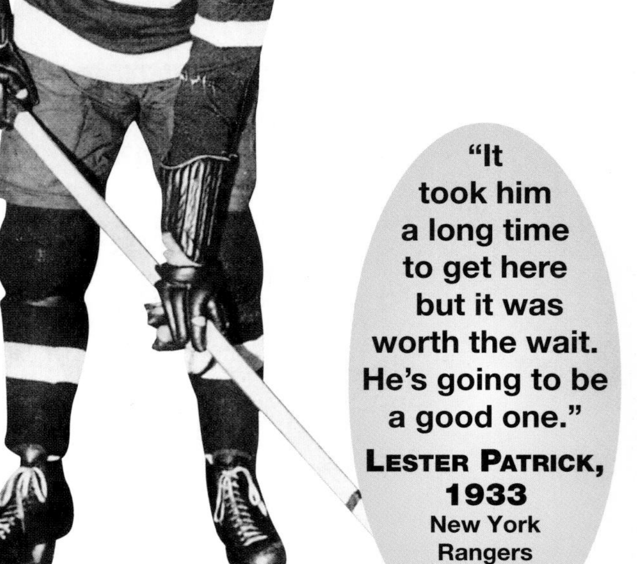

"It took him a long time to get here but it was worth the wait. He's going to be a good one."

Lester Patrick, 1933
New York Rangers general manager

Ken Dryden

Goalie — Montreal

Rookie Season	GP	W	L	T	SO	GAA
1971–72	64	39	8	15	8	2.24

Ken Dryden was one of the first players to continue his university education while playing hockey. In addition to being an excellent student of law and hockey, he had lightning reflexes and a long, lanky frame that seemed to fill the whole net. Dryden took rookie-of-the-year honours and led the NHL in wins and in minutes played in his rookie season. He went on to lead the Montreal Canadiens to six Stanley Cup titles — and earn a law degree.

"Dryden has already shattered the myth that college-raised skaters can't compete and that 6-foot-4-inch-tall athletes are too tall to fit into the mold of the ideal hockey player."

***Newsweek* Magazine, 1971**

Steve Larmer

Right Wing — Chicago, NY Rangers

Rookie Season	GP	G	A	TP	PIM
1982–83	80	43	47	90	28

Despite being only the 120th player selected in the 1980 Entry Draft, Steve Larmer was convinced he had the courage and talent to be a star in the NHL. He joined the Blackhawks as a regular in 1982 and played 884 consecutive games, playing even when he was injured. He became one of the lowest draft picks to earn the Calder Trophy and he set a Blackhawks rookie record by scoring 90 points.

"Not only is he scoring, but he's never out of position on his wing. In his own zone, he doesn't panic. He sees the situation and gets the job done."

Orval Tessier, 1982
Chicago Blackhawks coach

European Invasion

Salming recorded 39 points in his first season to set a Maple Leafs record for points by a rookie defenceman.

Borje Salming

Defence — Toronto, Detroit

Rookie Season	GP	G	A	TP	PIM
1973–74	76	5	34	39	48

Borje Salming was the first European-trained hockey player to become a star in the NHL. It wasn't easy. He encountered prejudice from players and fans who didn't want to see Europeans in the NHL. But Salming persevered. He refused to give up his dream of playing in the NHL. That courage opened the door for many other great players from across the ocean to play in North America.

Salming's puckhandling and skating skills set him apart from other rookies. Even as a first-year player, he made an impact with the Leafs and became the club's leader on both the power-play and penalty-killing units. Salming was a six-time All-Star for Toronto and holds the Maple Leafs records for career goals, assists and points by a defenceman.

"In the mid 1970s, it was Borje Salming who proved to the sceptics that European players had much to contribute to the North American game."
***Hockey: The Illustrated History,* 1985**

Peter Stastny

Centre — Quebec, New Jersey, St. Louis

Rookie Season	GP	G	A	TP	PIM
1980–81	77	39	70	109	37

Like all European hockey players, Peter Stastny had to adapt to a new culture and a new language in his rookie season in the NHL. But he had some advantages over other Europeans. His wife, children and brother also came to North America with him. As well, he was 24 years old and had already proved himself against the top talent in Europe.

"I didn't leave Czechoslovakia for the money. I didn't leave for the freedom. I left for the hockey."
PETER STASTNY, 1980

Stastny's effortless skating allowed him to reach full speed after only a couple of strides and easily outmanoeuvre the opposition. He shoots when goalies least expect it and is incredibly fast at getting shots away. He combined these talents with pinpoint passes to became the first rookie to register 100 points in a season. Stastny captured the Calder, and his rookie record for assists (70) still stands.

Peter and his brother, Anton, share the NHL record for points in a road game. Each scored eight points in a game against Washington on February 22, 1981.

Goaltending Greats

Ed Belfour

Goalie — Chicago

Rookie Season	GP	W	L	T	SO	GAA
1990–91	74	43	19	7	4	2.47

"Belfour has earned First Team All-Star honours wherever he has played: college, minor pro and the NHL."
***NHL Official Guide & Record Book,* 1991**

The road to success wasn't easy for Ed Belfour. No team drafted him and he spent two years in the minors before finally getting his chance to shine in the NHL. Belfour wasn't discouraged. He continued to work hard improving his reflexes and unorthodox style.

Belfour is a sprawling goalie who often dives across the crease to block shots. Playing this way, Belfour turned in one of the finest rookie seasons in NHL history. He led the NHL in games, wins and goals-against average. "Eddie the Eagle" also became the first goalie to win four individual honours: best goalie, rookie-of-the-year, fewest goals-against and the highest save percentage.

Belfour was the first goalie since Terry Sawchuk to win 40 games in his rookie season.

Tony Esposito

Goalie — Montreal, Chicago

Rookie Season	GP	W	L	T	SO	GAA
1969–70	63	38	17	8	15	2.17

In his first full season, Tony Esposito set a rookie record with 15 shutouts. No goalie, no matter how experienced, has matched that total in the past 25 years. That incredible performance earned him the Calder Trophy and the nickname "Tony O."

The key to Esposito's success was his leg strength. He spent hours running and biking to build up his leg muscles. He could drop to his knees, spreading his legs wide to protect the corners of the net, and still spring to his feet to snare pucks with his glove or sweep rebounds away with his stick. Tony O played 16 seasons in the NHL and accumulated 76 career shutouts.

"Tony will try to stop the puck with any part of his body at any time. I've seen him stop one with his mask. It wasn't luck, he actually put his face in front of the shot. He's a very brave goaltender."

Bobby Hull, 1971
Teammate

Tony O won the Stanley Cup with Montreal before winning the Calder with Chicago. (How's that possible? See page 4.)

The only goalie to beat Tony Esposito's mark of 15 shutouts was George Hainsworth, who had 22 shutouts in 1927–28.

The Complete Package

Lindros is one of only 13 rookies to score 40 goals in his first season in the NHL.

Eric Lindros

Centre — Philadelphia

Rookie Season	GP	G	A	TP	PIM
1992–93	61	41	34	75	147

Even before he had played a game in the NHL, scouts knew Eric Lindros was a complete player. He has all of the ingredients that make a superstar: size, speed, strength and smarts.

Lindros stands 193 cm (6 feet 4 inches) and weighs 107 kg (235 pounds). That size and strength enables him to deliver thundering open-ice body-checks or stand in the slot waiting for rebounds without being moved. He also has great acceleration. This allows him to retrieve loose pucks in the corner or soar around opposing defencemen as he makes a rink-long rush to the net.

But there is much more to the Lindros package. He is known as a "heads-up" player, which means he uses his brain as much as his body. Lindros anticipates where the puck will be before it even gets there. He can sense where his teammates are. These skills allowed him to become the first player ever to play for Team Canada in the Canada Cup tournament before playing in the NHL.

Although Lindros has been slowed by injuries in his first two seasons, he has still averaged well over a point per game. It is clear to every team in the NHL that this package delivers.

"Eric has great breakaway speed. He is unselfish and plays well with or without the puck. He has a thorough understanding of the game."
NHL Central Scouting Bureau, 1991

Lindros was named captain of the Flyers in the summer of 1994.

Hall of Fame Legends

Syl Apps

Centre — Toronto

Rookie Season	GP	G	A	TP	PIM
1936–37	48	16	29	45	10

Syl Apps was a champion pole-vaulter when he was discovered by Maple Leaf general manager Conn Smythe. Back in the 1930s, Smythe tried to get an edge on other teams by going beyond the obvious places when scouting for hockey players. He realized that hockey requires sharp reflexes, strength and endurance. Smythe quickly discovered that these qualities could often be found in lacrosse players and track-and-field stars.

Because of his track training, Apps had exceptional upper-body strength and a lightning-fast wrist shot. In his rookie season with the Leafs, he led the NHL in assists and took the Calder Trophy. A team player and one of the most gentlemanly ever, Apps was elected to the Hockey Hall of Fame in 1961.

"He is one of the very best to ever crash into the big time. He should be hailed as not only one of the top youngsters of this year but of several years."

J.P. Fitzgerald, 1937
Sportswriter

Apps represented Canada at the 1936 Olympic Games, finishing sixth in the pole vault.

Bernie Geoffrion

Right Wing — Montreal, NY Rangers

Rookie Season	GP	G	A	TP	PIM
1951–52	67	30	24	54	66

Bernie "Boom-Boom" Geoffrion became a legend because he was one of the first players to use a slapshot. That's how he earned his nickname. Geoffrion would spend hours in empty rinks practising the shot. As he slammed the puck against the end boards, a loud "boom-boom" would echo through the arena. This heavy shot helped Geoffrion score 30 goals in his first year and become rookie-of-the-year.

But there was more to Boom-Boom than his big shot. He was a flashy skater and a crushing body-checker who electrified the fans. In 1960–61, Geoffrion became the second player ever in NHL history to score 50 goals in a season (teammate Maurice "Rocket" Richard was the first). He was inducted into the Hall of Fame in 1972.

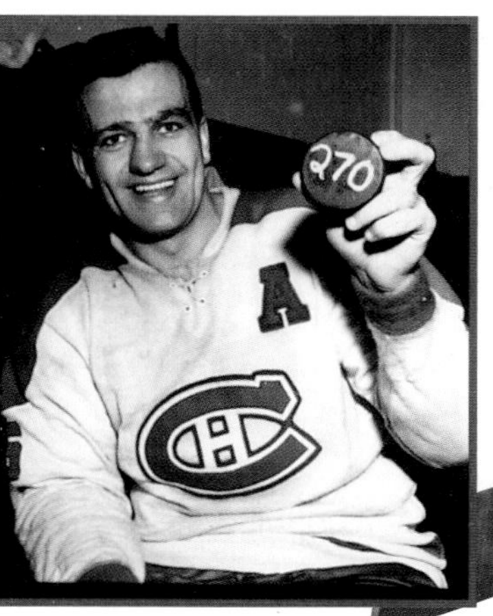

Geoffrion's 30 goals as a rookie was a record for first-year players that stood for almost 20 years.

"That kid is a better player than the Rocket was in his first season. He can do more things with the puck, stick-handle, skate both ways and take care of himself."

Dick Irvin, 1951
Montreal Canadiens coach

Future Phenoms

Jeff Friesen

Centre — San Jose
Rookie Season: 1994 – 95

Jeff Friesen is one of the Sharks' brightest young stars. He has break-out speed, a quick and accurate shot, and he's a talented playmaker. Friesen led the Canadian National Junior Team to a gold medal at the World Junior Championships in 1994 and 1995.

Todd Harvey

Centre — Dallas
Rookie Season: 1994 – 95

A solid, two-way player and on-ice leader, Todd Harvey was the Dallas Stars' first selection in the 1993 Entry Draft. Harvey has determination and discipline and he captained the Canadian National Junior Team that won the 1995 World Junior Championships.

Paul Kariya

Left Wing — Anaheim
Rookie Season: 1994 – 95

Not only is Paul Kariya a gifted puckhandler and crafty playmaker, but he is also already considered one of the game's quickest thinkers. In 1992–93, Kariya became the first college freshman to win the Hobey Baker Award as the top player in U.S. college hockey.